Meet the PEANUTS GANG!

WITH FUN FACTS, TRIVIA, COMICS, AND MORE!

based on the comic strip

PEANUTS

by Charles M. Schulz

Adapted by Natalie Shaw

Simon Spotlight
New York London Toronto Sydney New Delhi

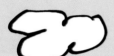

SIMON SPOTLIGHT
An imprint of Simon & Schuster Children's Publishing Division
1230 Avenue of the Americas, New York, New York 10020
First Simon Spotlight edition May 2015
© 2015 Peanuts Worldwide LLC
All rights reserved, including the right of reproduction in whole or in part in any form.
SIMON SPOTLIGHT and colophon are registered trademarks of Simon & Schuster, Inc.
For information about special discounts for bulk purchases, please contact
Simon & Schuster Special Sales at 1-866-506-1949 or business@simonandschuster.com.
Designed by Elizabeth Doyle
Manufactured in the United States of America 0415 LAK
10 9 8 7 6 5 4 3 2 1
ISBN 978-1-4814-3721-9
ISBN 978-1-4814-3722-6 (eBook)

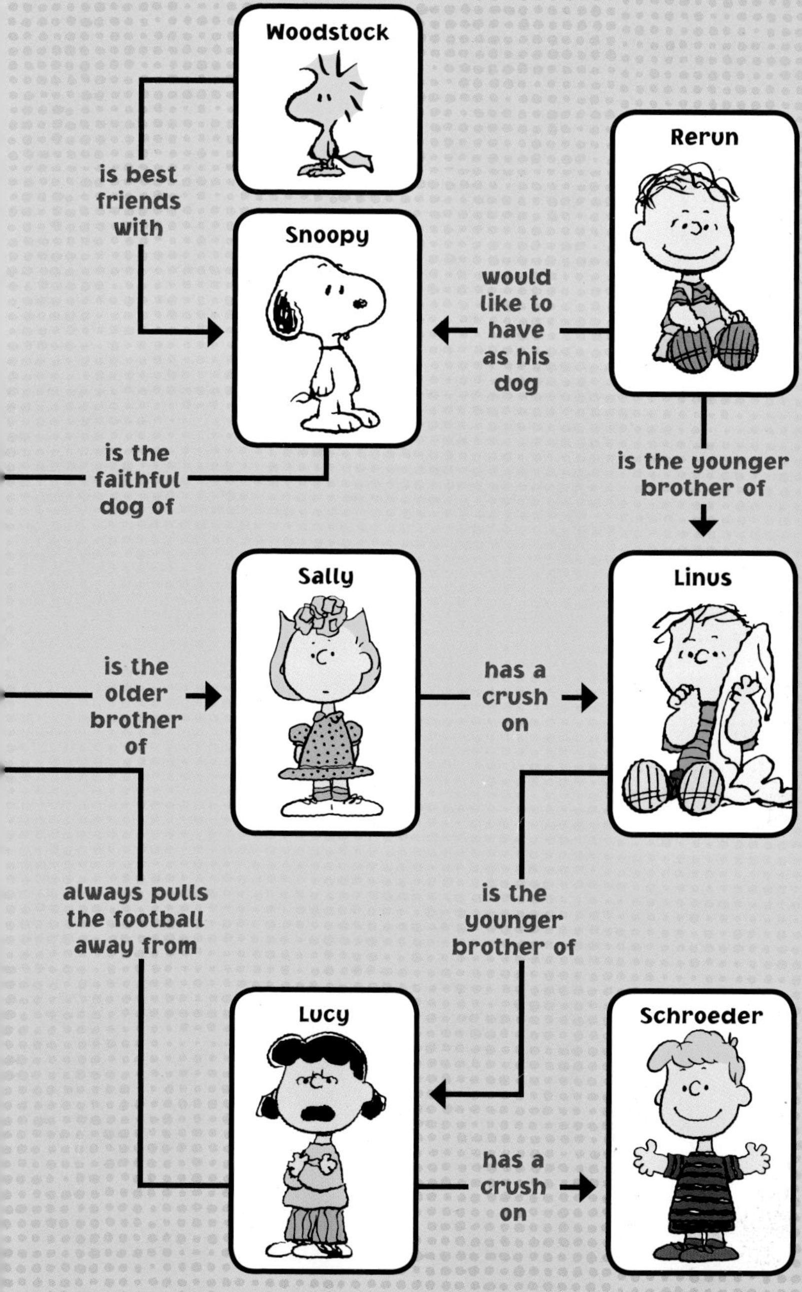
Woodstock
is best friends with
Snoopy
Rerun
would like to have as his dog
is the faithful dog of
is the younger brother of
Sally
Linus
is the older brother of
has a crush on
always pulls the football away from
is the younger brother of
Lucy
Schroeder
has a crush on

MEET THE PEANUTS GANG

Charlie Brown was introduced to the world in the very first Peanuts comic strip, published on October 2, 1950, and Snoopy followed soon after . . . but the boy and his iconic dog are just a couple of the characters in the Peanuts world.

There's bossy-but-loveable Lucy and her little brothers, Linus and Rerun. There's Peppermint Patty, a proud tomboy; Pigpen, who has his own personal dust cloud; the never seen Little Red-Haired Girl, the object of Charlie Brown's affection; and so many more.

They all came out of the imagination—and pen—of Charles M. Schulz. Did you know that Schulz's childhood dog, Spike, was the inspiration for Snoopy? Or how Charlie Brown's famous zigzag

shirt came to be? In this guide to the Peanuts characters, you'll get to know the stories, read the comics, and meet the whole neighborhood!

Charlie Brown's first appearance
October 2, 1950

WELL! HERE COMES OL' CHARLIE BROWN!
GOOD OL' CHARLIE BROWN....YES, SIR!
GOOD OL' CHARLIE BROWN...
HOW I HATE HIM!
SCHULZ

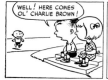

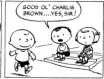

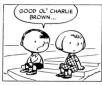

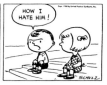

Snoopy's first appearance
October 4, 1950

?
SCHULZ

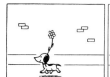

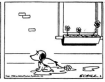

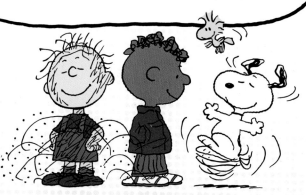

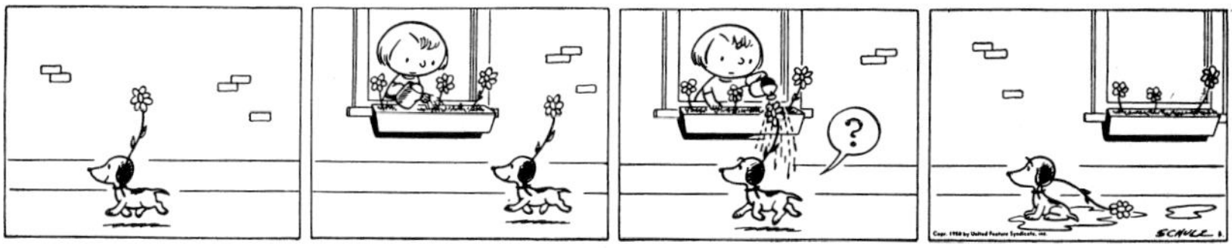

Schulz Says:

"ONE OF THE SECRETS OF A SUCCESSFUL COMIC STRIP IS NOT TO HAVE IT BASED ON THE PERSONALITY OF ONE CHARACTER. I REGARD THE COMIC STRIP LIKE THE KEYBOARD OF A PIANO: IF YOU KEEP PLAYING THE SAME NOTE OVER AND OVER, IT SOON BECOMES BORING, BUT IF YOU HAVE AN ENTIRE KEYBOARD TO PLAY, YOU CAN PRODUCE A GREAT VARIETY OF MUSIC."

CHARLIE BROWN

"Good Ol' Charlie Brown" is the star of the Peanuts world, the loveable loser in the zigzag shirt who never gives up (even though he almost never wins). While his friends think he's hopeless, he's the center of the comic strip universe. He manages the world's worst baseball team . . . yet shows up for every game. He can't muster up the courage to talk to the Little Red-Haired Girl . . . yet keeps hoping she'll fall for him. And although he gets grief from his friends, the Kite-Eating Tree, and even his own dog, Snoopy, Charlie Brown keeps on trying. He brings Snoopy his food every morning and night; watches out for his little sister, Sally; and stays friends with Lucy when she gives him a hard time. That's what pet owners, brothers, and friends are for!

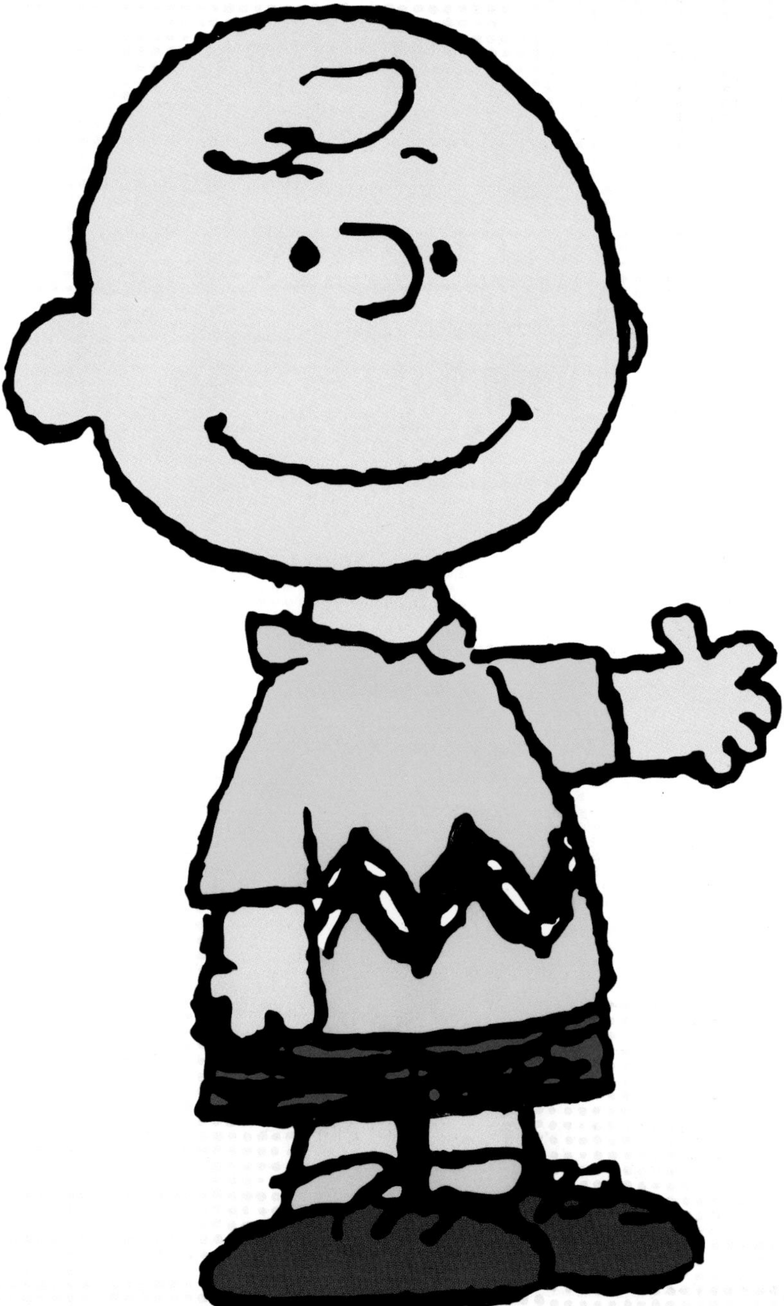

CATCHPHRASES

"Good grief!"

"I can't stand it! I just can't stand it!"

"Aaugh!"

THE KITE-EATING TREE

A lot of Charlie Brown's frustration is a direct result of the Kite-Eating Tree. Whenever he wants to fly a kite—one of his favorite things to do—the tree gets in his way. The second Charlie Brown tries to fly a kite, the tree gobbles it up! It has also eaten Linus's blanket and Schroeder's piano . . . when Lucy threw them into the tree out of spite.

DID YOU KNOW

- Charlie Brown's dad is a barber just like Charles Schulz's father.

- Charlie Brown's baseball team once lost a game by a score of 40 to 0. Charles Schulz's childhood team lost a game by the same score.

- In the beginning, Charlie Brown's shirt didn't have a zigzag stripe, but now he has a closet full of them that come in all sorts of colors including blue, red, and yellow.

IN CHARLIE BROWN'S OWN WORDS

"EVERYONE SHOULD START THE DAY WITH THIRTY PUSH-UPS!"

"IT'S NOT WISE TO LIE IN BED AT NIGHT ASKING YOURSELF QUESTIONS THAT YOU CAN'T ANSWER."

"LIFE IS GOING BY TOO FAST FOR ME. . . . STOP THE CLOCK!"

"THE WORLD IS FILLED WITH MONDAYS."

"GOOD-BYES ALWAYS MAKE MY THROAT HURT. . . . I NEED MORE HELLOS."

"IF YOU GRIT YOUR TEETH, AND SHOW REAL DETERMINATION, YOU ALWAYS HAVE A CHANCE!"

LIKES AND DISLIKES
LIKES

Baseball: As the manager and pitcher of his baseball team, he loves to play, but the team rarely scores any runs.

PEANUTS
GOOD GRIEF!

ONE HUNDRED AND EIGHTY-FOUR TO NOTHING!

I DON'T UNDERSTAND IT...

HOW CAN WE LOSE WHEN WE'RE SO SINCERE ?!

The Little Red-Haired Girl: He has a big crush on her, even though he's never had the courage to ask her name.

I THINK TOMORROW I'LL COME RIGHT OUT AND TELL THAT LITTLE RED-HAIRED GIRL THAT I LOVE HER..

THEN I'LL GIVE HER A BIG HUG..

THEN I'LL GO BUNGEE-JUMPING FROM THE MOON

CHARLIE BROWN
THROUGH THE AGES

"THERE'S NOT A COMIC STRIP CHARACTER THAT LOOKS TODAY AS IT DID WHEN THE STRIP FIRST BEGAN. EACH DAY YOU'RE TRYING TO DRAW IT THE BEST YOU CAN, AND YOU'RE NOT EVEN AWARE OF THE CHANGES."
—Charles Schulz

1950s

Kites: Charlie Brown loves flying kites, though he usually doesn't have much luck!

Writing to His Pen Pal: He often calls his pen pal his "pencil pal" because he has trouble writing with a pen.

His Dog, Snoopy: Charlie Brown is devoted to him, even though Snoopy rarely acts like a regular dog.

1960s   1970s   1980s   1990s

DISLIKES

Kicking a Football When Lucy Is Holding It: Charlie Brown *loves* kicking a football, but not when Lucy pulls it away every time!

Schulz Says:

On Losing

"CHARLIE BROWN MUST BE THE ONE WHO SUFFERS, BECAUSE HE'S A CARICATURE OF THE AVERAGE PERSON. MOST OF US ARE MUCH MORE ACQUAINTED WITH LOSING THAN WINNING. WINNING IS GREAT, BUT IT ISN'T FUNNY."

Names

"THE NAMES MOSTLY COME FROM FRIENDS. CHARLIE BROWN, FOR INSTANCE, IS NAMED AFTER A MAN I WORKED WITH AT AN ART SCHOOL IN MINNEAPOLIS. A MAN NAMED LINUS AND A WOMAN NAMED FRIEDA WORKED WITH US TOO. THOSE NAMES WENT INTO THE STRIP. BUT IT'S JUST THEIR NAMES I USE. I WOULD NEVER TAKE ANYONE'S CHARACTER."

The Zigzag Shirt

"I FIRST DREW CHARLIE BROWN JUST WEARING A WHITE T-SHIRT, BUT HE DIDN'T BOUNCE OFF THE PAGE. SO I GAVE HIM THAT LITTLE JAGGED STRIPE. . . . THE STRIPE SETS CHARLIE BROWN APART."

SALLY BROWN

Sally is Charlie Brown's little sister, and she is full of questions. Why does she have to go to school? And what's the capital of Venezuela? She is always on the hunt for answers. When she doesn't get them, she comes up with a new philosophy, asking "Who cares?" or "Why are you telling me?" Sally seems perpetually confused by the world. She mangles common speech and battles schoolteachers who refuse to appreciate her individuality. She's also rather greedy and wants to make sure that she receives her "fair share" . . . which often seems much larger than anybody else's. Sally is equally determined in her love for Linus, even though he doesn't like it when she calls him her "Sweet Babboo."

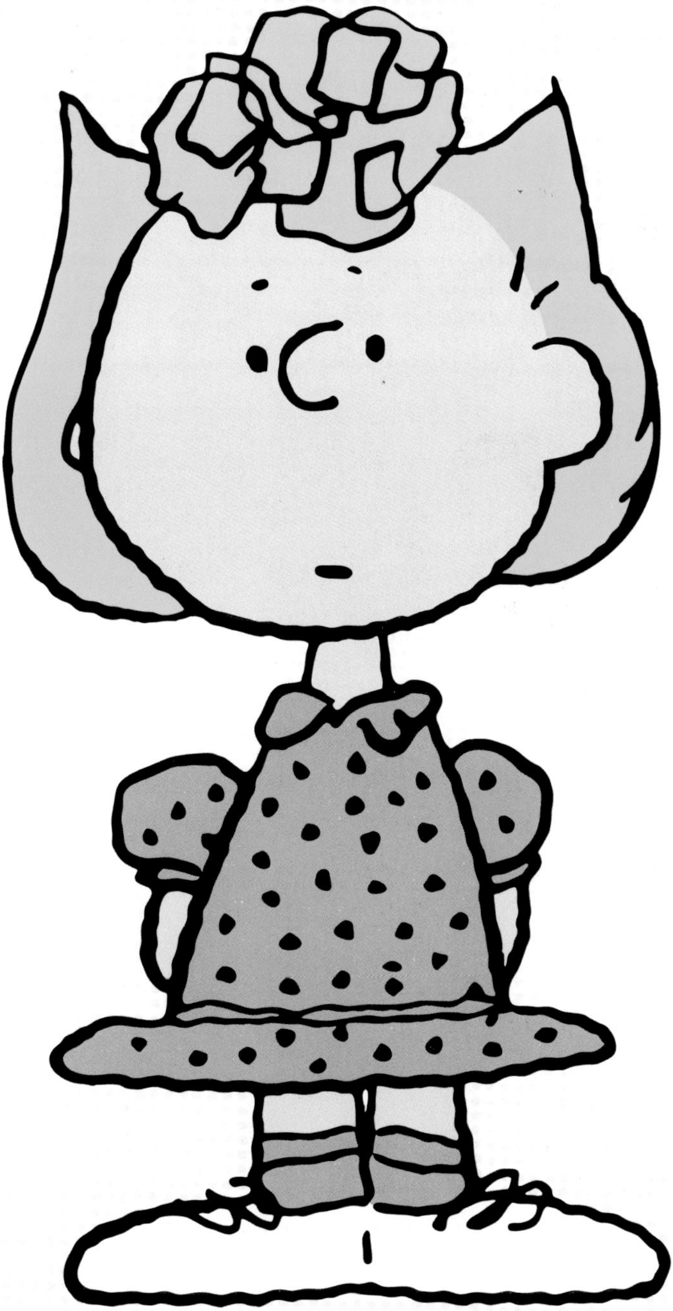

CATCHPHRASE

"Sweet Babboo."

DID YOU KNOW

• "Sweet Babboo," Sally's pet name for Linus, was inspired by Charles Schulz's wife, Jean. It's the same pet name she used for him!

• For six months, Sally had a lazy eye, also called amblyopia, and had to wear an eye patch.

PEANUTS

I SUPPOSE YOU'RE WONDERING WHY I'M WEARING THIS EYE PATCH, EH LINUS?

• Sally is known for often using the wrong word in her school reports.

• She calls Charlie Brown "Big Brother."

THE EARLY YEARS

When Sally was born on May 26, 1959, Charlie Brown was so excited to hear the news, he got a *little* confused:

This is what Sally looked like as a baby:

LIKES AND DISLIKES
LIKES

Her Philosophies: As soon as she chooses one, she finds another. . . .

Talking to the School Building: At least it listens to her!

Charlie Brown's Bedroom: Whenever her brother leaves the house, Sally tries to move into his bedroom!

I SEE YOU MADE IT HOME, BIG BROTHER..

I THOUGHT YOU WERE LOST FOR GOOD SO I MOVED A FEW OF MY THINGS INTO YOUR ROOM

THE BOOKS AND THE RECORD PLAYER WILL BE EASY TO MOVE BACK

THE DRESSER, THE COUCH, THE RUG, THE END TABLE, THE LAMP, THE BED AND THE MARTHA WASHINGTON CHAIR WILL TAKE A LITTLE LONGER

Linus: She is devoted to Linus, even though he doesn't love her back.

WE'LL SIT HERE IN THIS PUMPKIN PATCH, AND WHEN THE "GREAT PUMPKIN" FLIES OVER, WE'LL BE THE FIRST ONES TO SEE HIM!

THIS IS EXCITING, SWEET BABBOO!

DON'T CALL ME "SWEET BABBOO"!

THIS IS VERY SERIOUS!

OKAY, PUNKIN!

I CAN'T STAND IT!!

Getting Her Fair Share: To Sally, getting her fair share means getting *everything*.

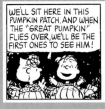

PEANUTS

I CAN'T GO THROUGH WITH IT!!

I HAVE TO GET CHRISTMAS PRESENTS! I WANT ALL I CAN GET, AND I WANT IT NOW BEFORE IT'S TOO LATE!

I WANT ALL I CAN GET BEFORE I'M TOO OLD, AND EVERYTHING IS GONE, AND THE SUN HAS DIMMED, AND THE STARS HAVE FALLEN, AND THE BIRDS ARE SILENT AND THE WHEAT IS EATEN...

"THE WHEAT IS EATEN"?

DISLIKES

School Papers and Reports: She might like them better if she did some reading!

The Start of Each School Year: She worries about everything from forgetting where her desk is to not knowing the capitals.

IN SALLY'S OWN WORDS

"LOVE MAKES YOU DO STRANGE THINGS."

"A GOOD PHILOSOPHY HELPS YOU ENDURE ALL OF THE TROUBLES WE HAVE IN LIFE."

"IF A PERSON HAS A NICE SMILE, NOTHING ELSE MATTERS."

"SOME PHILOSOPHIES TAKE A THOUSAND YEARS. . . . I THINK OF THEM IN TWO MINUTES."

SNOOPY

Snoopy is Charlie Brown's dog, but it might be more accurate to say that Charlie Brown is Snoopy's person. The world-famous beagle has a sassy streak that often gets him into trouble. He started out life as a puppy at the Daisy Hill Puppy Farm and eventually found a home with Charlie Brown. Although he behaved as a regular dog during the early years of Peanuts, Snoopy eventually started walking on his hind legs; doing happy dances; and imagining himself as a World-Famous Writer, Joe Cool, the Flying Ace, and more. A dog might usually be a man's best friend, but Snoopy is more faithful to his feathered sidekick, Woodstock, than to his devoted owner. He's a dog with a mind—and an imagination—of his own. At the end of each day, though, Snoopy needs Charlie Brown as much as Charlie Brown needs him. "Nothing is more comforting," Charlie Brown once said, "than sitting with your faithful dog in your lap." Snoopy would probably agree, except to state that he prefers to sit with his chin resting on Charlie Brown's round head!

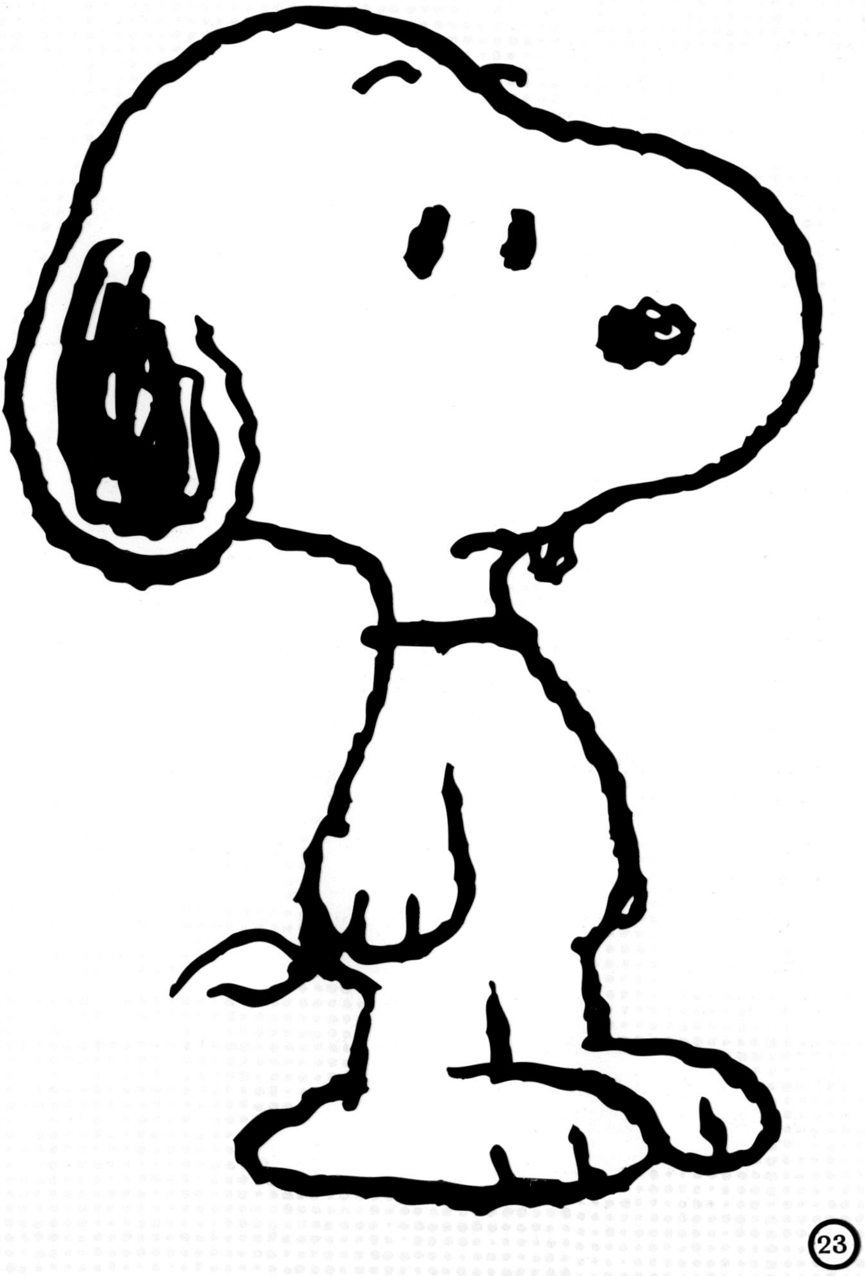

CATCHPHRASE

"That round-headed kid."
(When he's thinking about
Charlie Brown.)

Schulz Says:

"SNOOPY REFUSES TO BE CAUGHT IN THE
TRAP OF DOING ORDINARY THINGS LIKE
CHASING AND RETRIEVING STICKS."

"I PATTERNED SNOOPY IN APPEARANCE AFTER A DOG
I HAD WHEN I WAS ABOUT THIRTEEN YEARS OLD. HIS
NAME WAS SPIKE, AND HE LOOKED A LITTLE BIT LIKE THE
ORIGINAL SNOOPY. BUT SNOOPY DIDN'T START OFF BEING
A BEAGLE. IT'S JUST THAT 'BEAGLE' IS A FUNNY WORD."

DID YOU KNOW

• Charlie Brown wasn't Snoopy's first owner. It was a girl named Lila who brought Snoopy home, only to discover that her family's building didn't allow dogs. Lila writes to Snoopy and sends him Valentines, and when she was in the hospital, Snoopy went to visit her.

• Snoopy's doghouse once burned down and was rebuilt. The inside of his doghouse has never been shown in the comic, but it seems to hold much more than it should, given its size.

• Snoopy reads *War and Peace* at the rate of one word a day.

LIKES AND DISLIKES
LIKES

Lying on His Back on the Roof of His Doghouse: This is where he looks for shapes in the clouds and sits with his friend Woodstock lying on his belly.

Woodstock: Snoopy is devoted to his little feathered friend.

SNOOPY
THROUGH THE AGES

"IT TOOK ALMOST TEN YEARS FOR SNOOPY TO GET UP ON HIS HIND FEET AND WALK AROUND LIKE A CARTOON DOG . . . AND PROBABLY ANOTHER TEN YEARS FOR HIM TO THINK THE THOUGHTS THAT HE NOW DOES. THAT'S THE WAY COMIC STRIPS GO."

—Charles Schulz

1950s

Doing His "Happy Dance": Which is not to be confused with his "Second Day of May Dance," his "Happy New Year Dance," or his "Ha-Ha . . . You Have to Go to School and I Don't! Dance"!

DISLIKES

The Cat Next Door: Snoopy is afraid of the cat next door, and for good reason. The cat is never pictured, but it has large, sharp claws.

1960s   1970s   1980s   1990s

SNOOPY'S ALTER EGOS

Snoopy has a big imagination, and has adopted more than one hundred personas. As Joe Cool, he's the hip college hound. As the World War I Flying Ace, he flies a plane, battling the notorious Red Baron. While pondering life from the top of his doghouse, he writes The Great American Novel, travels to the moon, and more.
His most famous alter egos are:

JOE COOL

As Joe Cool, Snoopy slips on shades and oozes charm, at least in his imagination. He hangs around the college dorm and student union, trying to talk to "chicks" and wishes he had wheels (a car). He also says things like "That's a drag" and "No way," even when he's interested in something.

THE WORLD WAR I FLYING ACE

As the Flying Ace, Snoopy flies through the air in his Sopwith Camel (his doghouse) to take on the dreaded Red Baron over war-torn France. The Red Baron is never pictured, but he often shoots the doghouse full of holes.

THE WORLD-FAMOUS AUTHOR

Snoopy likes being the world's best at anything he sets his mind to. If he is going to write a novel, it will be the world's *best* novel . . . if he can just get past the opening line, "It was a dark and stormy night."

BEAGLE SCOUT LEADER

As a Beagle Scout, Snoopy leads his troupe of scouts (Woodstock and his bird buddies) on long treks and adventures. But on his first hike, before the Beagle Scouts joined him, he got lost in part because he thought the N on his compass meant "nowhere" instead of "North"!

Schulz Says:

"HE'S A VERY STRONG CHARACTER: HE CAN WIN OR LOSE, BE A DISASTER, A HERO, OR ANYTHING, AND YET IT ALL WORKS OUT. I LIKE THE FACT THAT WHEN HE'S IN REAL TROUBLE, HE CAN RETREAT INTO A FANTASY AND THEREBY ESCAPE."

MORE ALTER EGOS

World-Famous Astronaut: Snoopy went where no beagle has gone before!

Helicopter: Snoopy can turn his ears into propeller blades.

World-Famous Surgeon: Snoopy struts in scrubs and heads to the golf course to blow off steam after surgery!

The Head Beagle: Purely an administrative position (and a thankless one at that), Snoopy had a short stint in an office as the Head Beagle.

French Foreign Legion Officer: Snoopy patrols the desert sands as a foreign legion officer.

World-Famous Attorney: Snoopy will mount a fierce defense for a plate full of cookies.

The Easter Beagle: Snoopy does his happy dance to usher in the spring and doles out Easter eggs.

LUCY VAN PELT

Lucy is known around the neighborhood for being crabby, bossy, and a fussbudget—she always finds a reason to complain. She has a sharp tongue, and she isn't afraid to use it. Whether she's happily listing all of Charlie Brown's faults or forcing her little brother Linus to give up his blanket, Lucy always believes she is right. She even runs her own psychiatrist's booth for a profit, even though she only charges five cents! She plays a running joke on Charlie Brown, offering to hold a football while he kicks it, only to pull away the ball at the last second. Lucy's one weakness? Her unrequited love for the piano-playing Schroeder. Unfortunately, he tends to ignore her, even when she's draped at the foot of his piano.

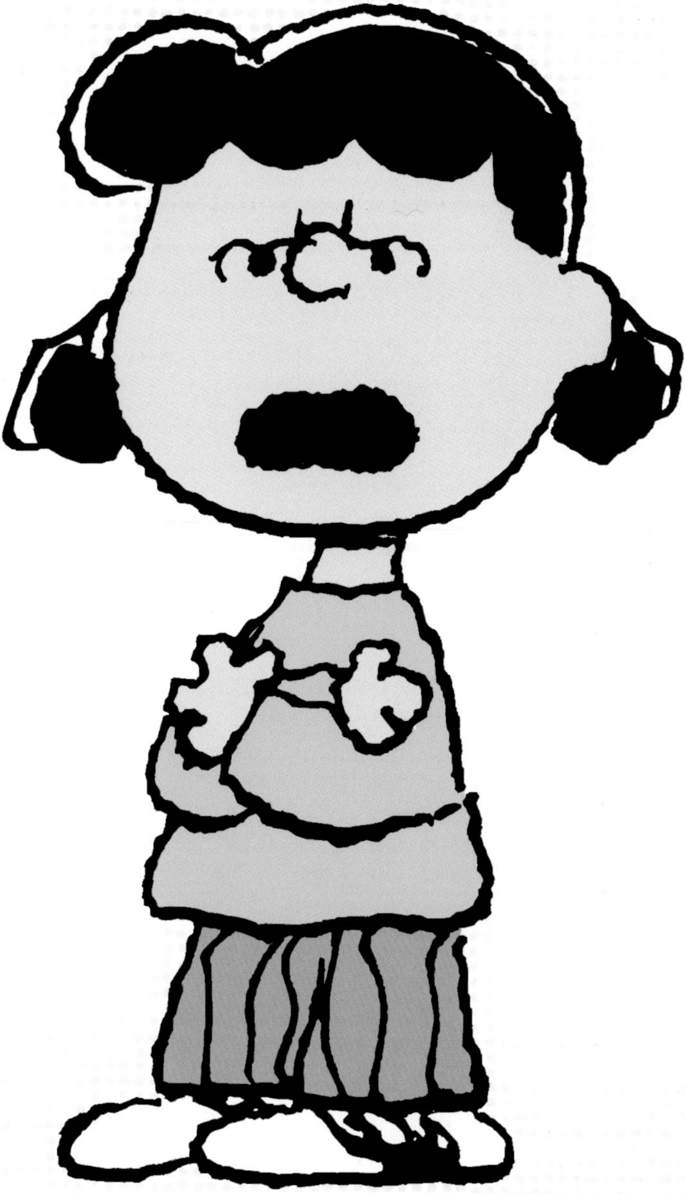

CATCHPHRASE

"You blockhead!"

DID YOU KNOW

• Lucy often speaks out for women's rights and aspires to one day be president and queen.

• Her signature footwear is black-and-white saddle shoes.

Schulz Says:

"LUCY COMES FROM THAT PART OF ME THAT'S CAPABLE OF SAYING MEAN AND SARCASTIC THINGS, WHICH IS NOT A GOOD TRAIT TO HAVE, SO LUCY GIVES ME A GOOD OUTLET. BUT EACH CHARACTER HAS A WEAKNESS, AND LUCY'S WEAKNESS IS SCHROEDER. WITH SCHROEDER, EVEN LUCY HAS MOMENTS OF SENTIMENTALITY, LIKE THE TIME SHE ASKED HIM WHY HE NEVER SENT HER FLOWERS AND HE SAID, 'BECAUSE I DON'T LIKE YOU.' AND SHE ANSWERED, 'THE FLOWERS WOULDN'T CARE.'"

"NOW ABOUT LUCY BEING SO MEAN. SHE IS MEAN FIRST BECAUSE IT IS FUNNY, AND BECAUSE IT JUST FOLLOWS THE STANDARD COMIC STRIP PATTERN THAT THE SUPPOSEDLY WEAK PEOPLE IN THE WORLD ARE FUNNY WHEN THEY DOMINATE THE SUPPOSEDLY STRONG PEOPLE."

LUCY'S PSYCHIATRIST'S BOOTH

Unlike most children, who have lemonade stands, Lucy can often be found dispensing advice from her five-cent psychiatrist's booth. Today, as usual, the doctor is in! But beware. . . . While she offers up some useful words of wisdom, she is also known for giving terrible advice.

"EACH GENERATION MUST BE ABLE TO BLAME THE PREVIOUS GENERATION FOR ITS PROBLEMS."

"STOP COMPLAINING. . . . GETTING UP EARLY IN THE MORNING IS GOOD FOR YOU."

"THERE ARE SO MANY THINGS IN LIFE THAT WE CAN NEVER BE SURE ABOUT."

PSYCHIATRIC HELP 5¢

"WE LEARN MORE FROM LOSING THAN WE DO FROM WINNING."

"I THINK EVERY WEEK SHOULD HAVE ONE DAY IN IT WHEN BOYS GIVE PRESENTS TO GIRLS."

THE DOCTOR IS **IN**

LIKES AND DISLIKES
LIKES

Schroeder: Lucy shows her sweet side by sitting at his piano, trying to get his attention.

Giving Advice: Her psychiatrist's booth is a win-win; Lucy gets to be bossy *and* get paid for it!

Being Bossy: Maybe it's because she's a big sister, but Lucy takes bossiness to another level.

LUCY
THROUGH THE AGES

"I LIKE LUCY BECAUSE OF THE FACT THAT SHE PROVIDES ME WITH SO MANY IDEAS. I DON'T NECESSARILY APPROVE OF HER PERSONALITY. . . ."
—Charles Schulz

1950s

DISLIKES

Playing Baseball: But in spite of Charlie Brown's begging, she refuses to quit the team.

HEY, MANAGER, ARE WE SUPPOSED TO YELL, "I GOT IT!" OR "I HAVE IT!"?

IT DOESN'T MATTER, LUCY

I THINK HE'S RIGHT

IF YOU DON'T GOT IT, YOU DON'T HAVE IT!

Having Brothers: She always wanted a sister!

2-24

HOW CAN ANY PERSON BE EXPECTED TO LIVE IN THE SAME HOUSE WITH TWO BROTHERS?!!

WHAT KIND OF A QUESTION WAS THAT?

Dog Lips: Of course, that makes Snoopy try his hardest to kiss her every chance he gets.

PEANUTS
IT WASN'T A FAIR FIGHT! HE KISSED ME!

HE KISSED ME WITH HIS STUPID DOG LIPS!!
BLEAH!

I'M STILL THE "ARM WRESTLING" CHAMP OF THE NEIGHBORHOOD!

YOU LET US DOWN, "MASKED MARVEL"
SORRY, BOYS...THAT'S THE WAY IT GOES....

1960s

1970s

1980s

1990s

LINUS
VAN PELT

Linus is the thoughtful neighborhood philosopher who always has a kind word for everybody . . . even his bossy older sister, Lucy. He might sound all grown-up, but he doesn't go anywhere without clutching his dear security blanket. He is also the smartest kid on the block (though he would never admit it) and is Charlie Brown's best friend and his second baseman on the baseball team. Linus is a true believer, whether it's believing the outrageous whoppers that Lucy passes off as "educated facts" or trying in vain, every October, to persuade his friends to celebrate the arrival of the Great Pumpkin, who Linus believes brings toys to children on Halloween. Like all those who believe the best of the world, however, Linus suffers more than most when people (or pumpkins) let him down.

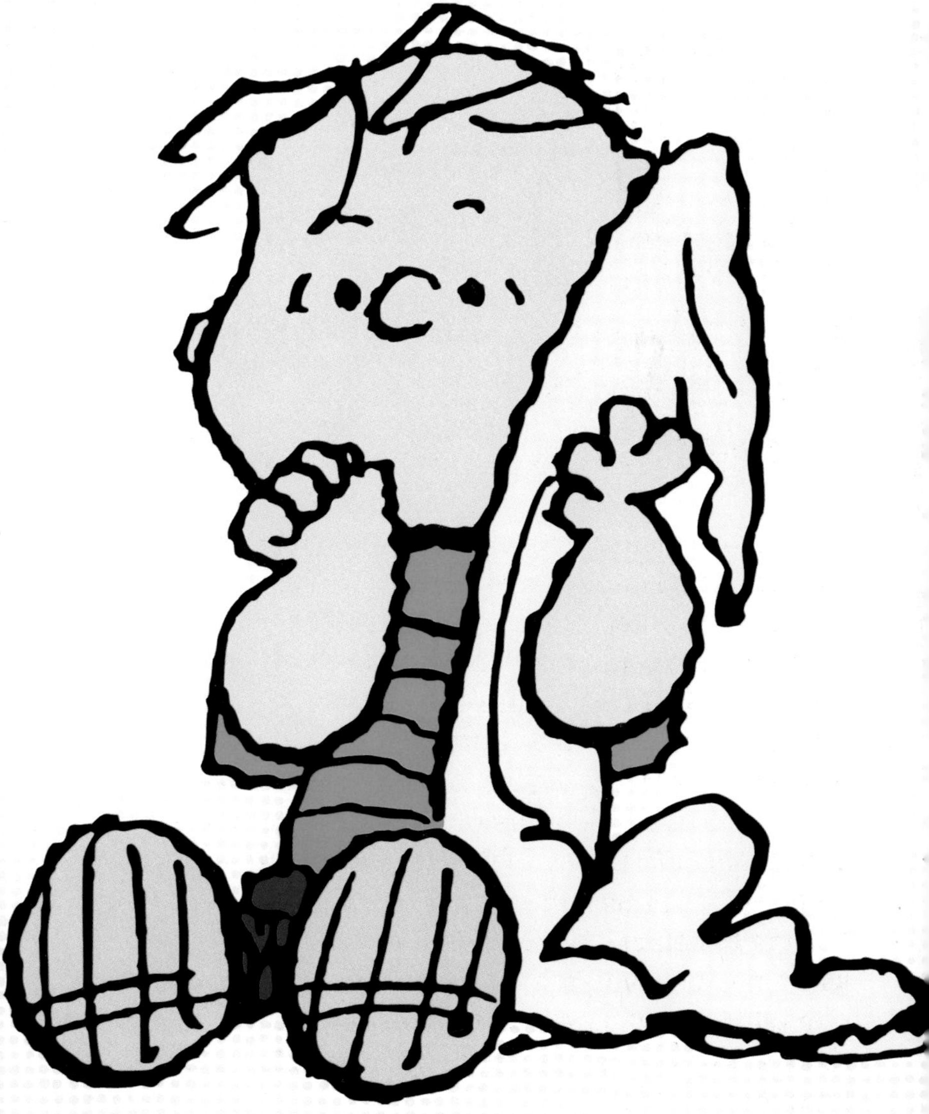

CATCHPHRASE

**"Happiness is . . .
a warm blanket."**

DID YOU KNOW

• Linus wore glasses for a short time. Snoopy constantly stole them to torment him.

• Lucy once turned Linus's blanket into a kite.

• Snoopy likes to grab on to an end of Linus's blanket and start running . . . while Linus holds on for dear life!

Schulz Says:

"LINUS IS STRONG ENOUGH TO CARRY A STRIP BY HIMSELF. HIS BIGGEST WEAKNESS, OF COURSE, IS THE BLANKET. BUT HE'S VERY BRIGHT. . . . LINUS'S PROBLEM IS THAT HE'S UNDER THE THUMB OF THIS DOMINATING SISTER AND A MOTHER WHO PUTS NOTES IN HIS LUNCH TELLING HIM TO STUDY HARDER. AS CHARLIE BROWN SAYS, 'NO WONDER HE CARRIES THAT BLANKET.' I LIKE TO WORK WITH LINUS. HE'S A NEAT CHARACTER."

IN LINUS'S OWN WORDS

"IT'S SURPRISING WHAT YOU CAN ACCOMPLISH WITH A LITTLE SMOOTH TALKING AND SOME FAST ACTION!"

"NEVER SET YOUR STOMACH FOR A JELLY-BREAD SANDWICH UNTIL YOU'RE SURE THERE'S SOME JELLY!"

"LIFE IS MORE PLEASANT WHEN YOU HAVE SOMETHING TO LOOK FORWARD TO."

"WITH MY BLANKET IN HAND AND THE SYMPATHY OF MY FRIENDS, I CANNOT FAIL!"

"THERE'S A GOOD FEELING TO BE HAD FROM SHARING."

"DOGS ACCEPT PEOPLE FOR WHAT THEY ARE."

LIKES AND DISLIKES
LIKES

His Beloved Security Blanket: It comes second only to sucking his thumb.

Being the Neighborhood Philosopher: Someone's got to do it!

The Great Pumpkin: Linus believes wholeheartedly in the Great Pumpkin, even though no one else does.

LINUS
THROUGH THE AGES

"LINUS CAME FROM A DRAWING THAT I MADE ONE DAY OF A FACE ALMOST LIKE THE ONE HE NOW HAS. I EXPERIMENTED WITH SOME WILD HAIR, AND I SHOWED THE SKETCH TO A FRIEND OF MINE WHO SAT NEAR ME AT THE CORRESPONDENCE SCHOOL, WHOSE NAME WAS LINUS MAURER. HE THOUGHT IT WAS KIND OF FUNNY, AND WE BOTH AGREED THAT IT MIGHT MAKE A GOOD NEW CHARACTER FOR THE STRIP."

—Charles Schulz

1950s

Outwitting His Sister, Lucy: Usually in very creative ways.

DISLIKES

Notes in His Lunch Box: That might be because they're always notes from his mom about how he needs to live up to her expectations.

Unwanted Attention from Sally:

Linus always proclaims: "I am not your Sweet Babboo!"

960   1970s   1980s   990

RERUN
VAN PELT

The youngest Van Pelt, Rerun, spends a lot of time riding on the back of his mother's bicycle, hoping to avoid falling into potholes and being flattened by semitrucks. Rerun takes after his brother, Linus, and is introspective, but he doesn't need a security blanket. He wants nothing more than to put baby stuff behind him and grow up— literally. He perceives a world of opportunities and experiences that are beyond him solely because of his size: everything from having his own dog to being able to interact with the big kids in a variety of sporting activities. Rerun approaches life with zeal, whether it's creating underground comics for his kindergarten class or attempting to dunk on the basketball court. Life—with all its complexities and mysteries—is just unfolding for this little guy, and he wants to be ready for anything.

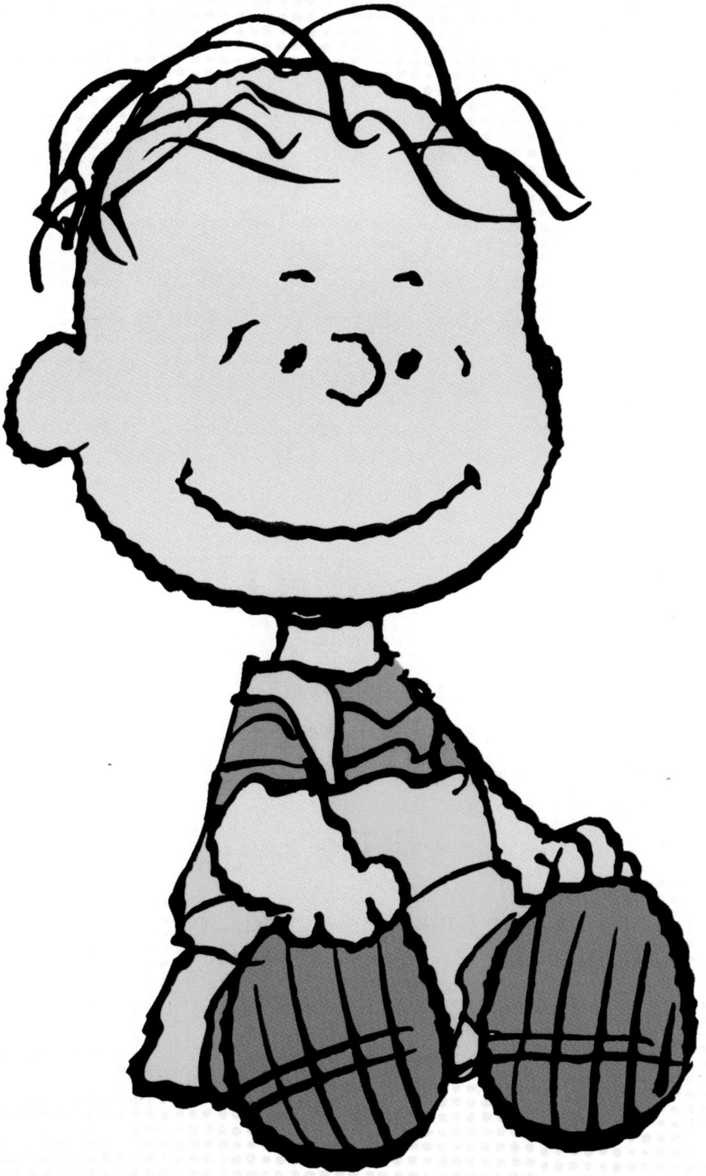

DID YOU KNOW

• Lucy and Linus are the ones who named their baby brother Rerun. He doesn't hold it against them!

Schulz Says:

"RERUN IS MORE SKEPTICAL THAN HIS BROTHER, MUCH HARDER TO CONVINCE, AND ALWAYS GETS AROUND LUCY WHERE LINUS GIVES IN."

LIKES AND DISLIKES

LIKES

Being the Baby of the Family: That said, he is a bit jaded.

Cookies: And other simple pleasures of childhood.

DISLIKES

Riding on the Back of His Mom's Bicycle: Maybe because he has to hold on for dear life!

Being Too Little: He wants to play sports like the older kids!

PEPPERMINT PATTY

A fearless leader and a natural athlete, Peppermint Patty is up to any challenge . . . except studying. She never met a school day she didn't hate. But this tough girl has a soft side too: She's hopelessly in love with her pal Charlie "Chuck" Brown—who has no idea. For Peppermint Patty, sports are easy; it's life that's hard. Peppermint Patty lives in a different neighborhood from Charlie Brown, Snoopy, and the gang, but she goes to the same school as Franklin and her best friend, Marcie. She lives with her dad, who's a single father. Baseball, football, and ice-skating are just a few of the sports she excels at and just one of the reasons her dad always calls her "his rare gem."

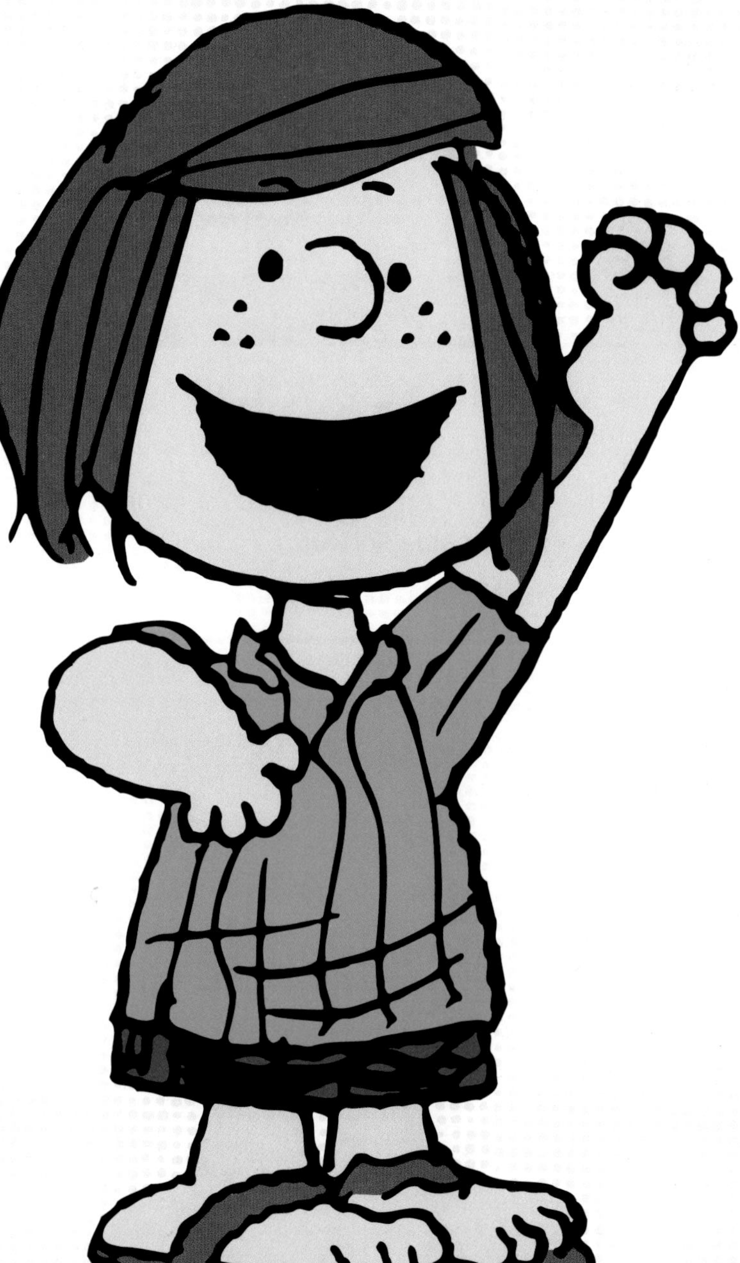

CATCHPHRASE

"Stop calling me 'sir'!"

(to Marcie)

DID YOU KNOW

- Peppermint Patty's real name is Patricia Reichardt.
- She met her best friend, Marcie, at summer camp, but they go to the same school.
- She loves ice-skating as much as she loves team sports.

PEPPERMINT PATTY'S NICKNAMES

"Peppermint Patty" likes to give nicknames to her friends:

- "Chuck" is her nickname for Charlie Brown.
- "Lucille" is her nickname for Lucy.
- "That Funny-Looking Kid" or "That Funny-Looking Kid with the Big Nose" are her nicknames for Snoopy.

Schulz Says:

"OTHER CHARACTERS ARE THERE MERELY TO FILL ROLES WHEN THEY ARE NEEDED. EXCEPT FOR PEPPERMINT PATTY. I PUT HER IN BECAUSE THAT'S A GREAT NAME, AND I DIDN'T WANT TO LOSE IT, BECAUSE ANOTHER CARTOONIST MIGHT THINK OF IT."

IN PEPPERMINT PATTY'S OWN WORDS

"SUBTRACTION IS THE AWFUL FEELING THAT YOU KNOW LESS TODAY THAN YOU DID YESTERDAY."

"THERE SEEM TO BE MORE QUESTIONS THAN ANSWERS . . . SO TRY TO BE THE ONE WHO ASKS THE QUESTIONS!"

LIKES AND DISLIKES

LIKES

Her Friend Marcie: Except when Marcie calls her "sir," which is all the time.

Sports of All Kinds: But she assumes everyone likes sports as much as she does.

Charlie Brown: She has a crush on him, but often denies it.

Defeating Charlie Brown's Baseball Team: She loves winning games.

DISLIKES

Getting Her Ears Pierced: Mostly because she ended up with only one ear pierced!

School: She might like it better if she didn't get straight D minuses for grades.

Her Appearance: Peppermint Patty doesn't believe she is beautiful until Marcie's mother gives her a dress to wear for an ice-skating competition.

MARCIE

Marcie is Peppermint Patty's best friend, loyal follower, and complete opposite. She's horrible at sports but terrific at friendship, especially with Charlie Brown, who she calls "Charles," and Peppermint Patty, who she calls "sir." Where Peppermint Patty struggles to get even D minuses in class, Marcie is a whiz, and while Peppermint Patty hits home runs, Marcie can't tell the difference between baseball and hockey. Marcie always does her homework well (and quickly) and always knows the right answer when she gets called on in class. But she doesn't flaunt her knowledge; she goes out of her way to help the other kids figure out the right answers. Marcie is one of the sweetest kids in the neighborhood.

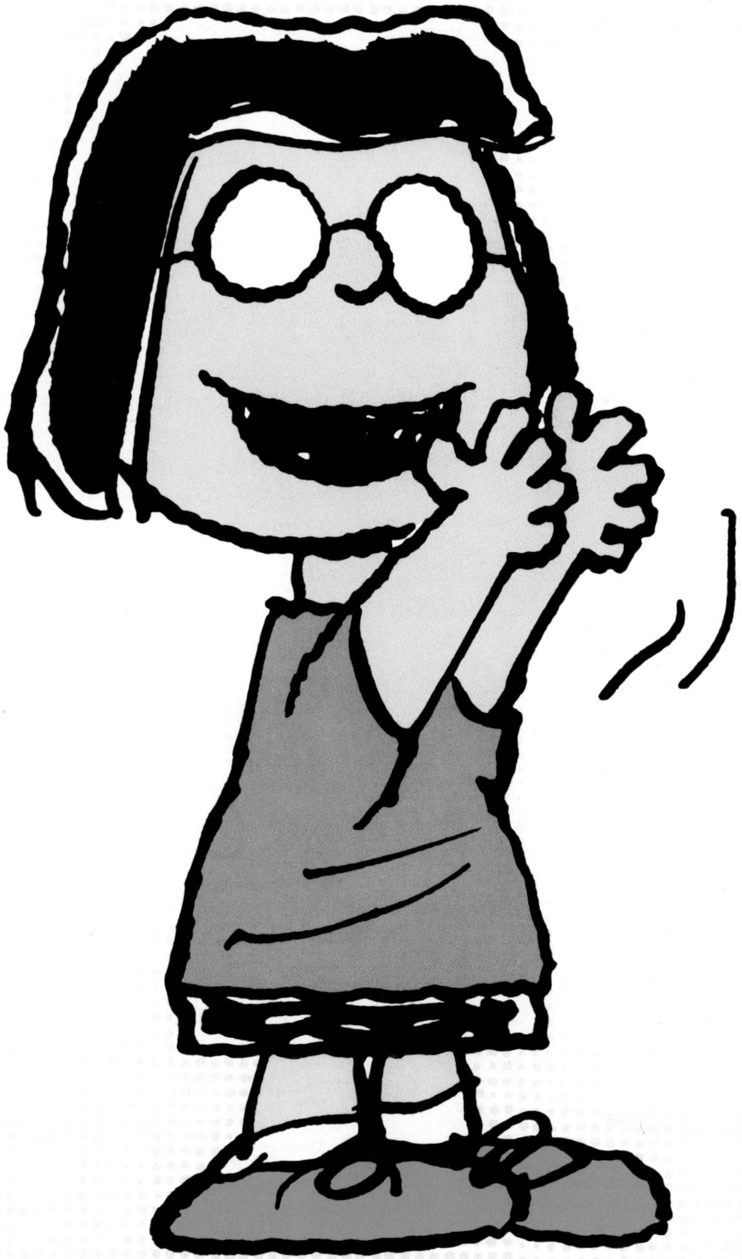

LIKES AND DISLIKES
LIKES

Calling Peppermint Patty "Sir": Marcie does this again and again, unaware that it bothers her friend.

School, Reading, Learning, and Studying: She loves anything to do with learning.

Charlie Brown: She has a crush on Charlie Brown too. It might be the one thing she and Peppermint Patty have in common.

DISLIKES

The Fact That Peppermint Patty Doesn't Like School: She spends a lot of her time trying to convince her to go!

Sports of All Kinds: Marcie hates sports as much as Peppermint Patty loves sports.

Schulz Says:

"I LOVE THE LITTLE RELATIONSHIP, WHICH TOOK A LONG TIME TO DEVELOP, BETWEEN MARCIE AND PEPPERMINT PATTY. THEY INSULT EACH OTHER ALL THE TIME, YET THEY STILL APPRECIATE EACH OTHER."

SCHROEDER

A mini musical genius, Schroeder is rarely separated from his incredibly versatile toy piano or his idol, Beethoven. Everything—school, girls, summer camp—takes a backseat to his daily regimen of piano practice. The only exception is when he's calling a game as a reliable catcher on Charlie Brown's baseball team. Schroeder tries (with limited success) to signal the proper pitch, only to watch as the opposing team fires another line drive right over the pitcher's mound. The rest of his time is spent fending off unwanted advances from Lucy, who parks herself at the end of his piano and talks about the happy life they might share . . . a dream in her mind, a nightmare in his. If only she could understand, music is his true love!

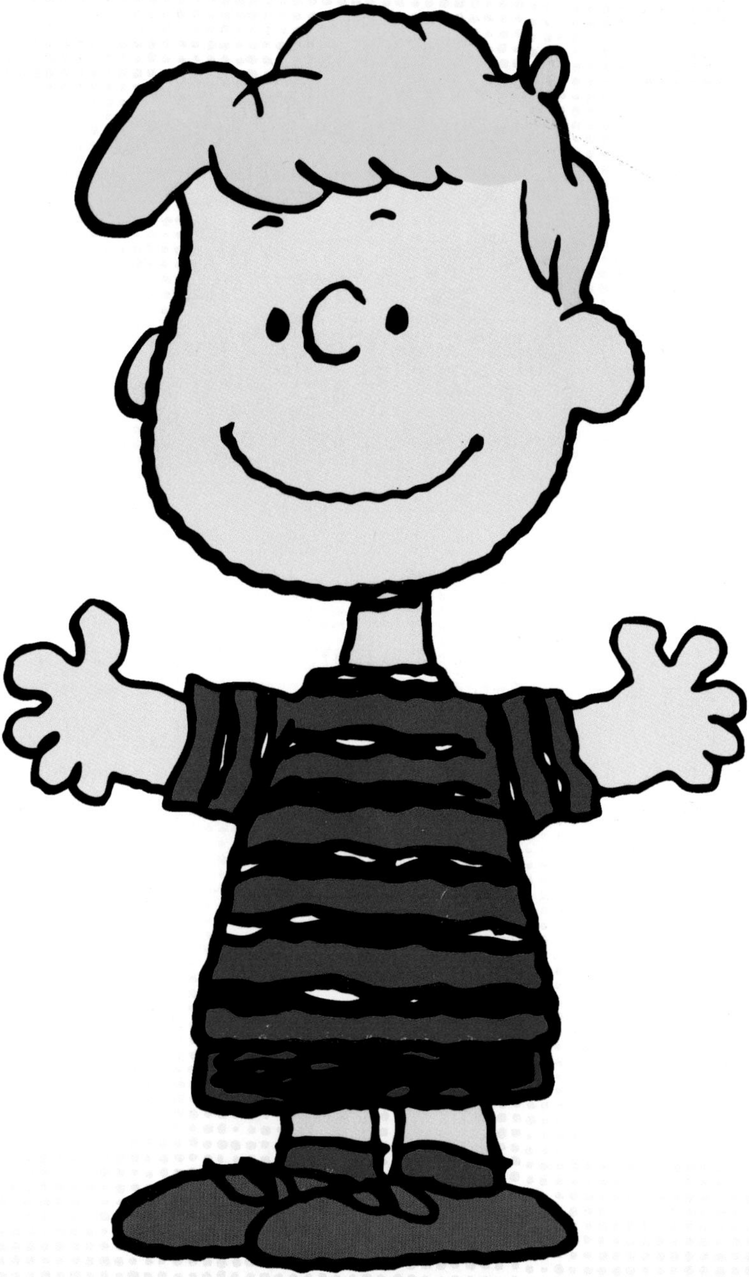

DID YOU KNOW

• Schulz chose Beethoven as Schroeder's muse because he believed words beginning with B sounded funny . . . like "blockhead" and "beagle."

• Schroeder believes Beethoven was the first president of the United States and that his birthday should be a national holiday!

• Snoopy sometimes interacts with Schroeder's music notes in a way that isn't humanly—or caninely—possible.

THE EARLY YEARS

Schroeder first appeared in the comic strip as a baby, and Charlie Brown is the one who first showed him a piano. For Schroeder and the piano, it was love at first sight . . .

Schulz Says:

"SCHROEDER WAS NAMED AFTER A YOUNG BOY WITH WHOM I USED TO CADDY AT A GOLF COURSE IN ST. PAUL. I DON'T RECALL EVER KNOWING HIS FIRST NAME, BUT JUST 'SCHROEDER' SEEMED RIGHT FOR THE CHARACTER IN THE STRIP EVEN BEFORE HE BECAME THE GREAT MUSICIAN HE NOW IS."

LIKES AND DISLIKES
LIKES

Beethoven: "Like" isn't a strong enough word for Schroeder's feelings for his idol, Beethoven.

Playing Music on His Toy Piano: Even when Snoopy gets in the way!

Baseball: He's a catcher on Charlie Brown's baseball team.

DISLIKES

Lucy's Affection for Him: She refuses to believe they aren't meant to be together. He refuses to like her.

FRANKLIN

Franklin is Charlie Brown's quiet friend and confidant. Along with Linus, Franklin is one of the few Peanuts characters who never pokes fun at Charlie Brown. In fact, Franklin never has an unkind word for anybody; like Marcie, he's genuinely thoughtful and kind. He lives in a different neighborhood from Charlie Brown and most of his friends, so he attends a different school and plays on a different baseball team. When he visits Charlie Brown's neighborhood, he takes the weirdness of that beagle, the girl with the psychiatrist's booth, and the kid with the blanket with a grain of salt. In the comic strips where Charlie Brown is seen standing behind a wall, voicing his doubts and philosophies, Franklin is often there, lending an ear to his friend.

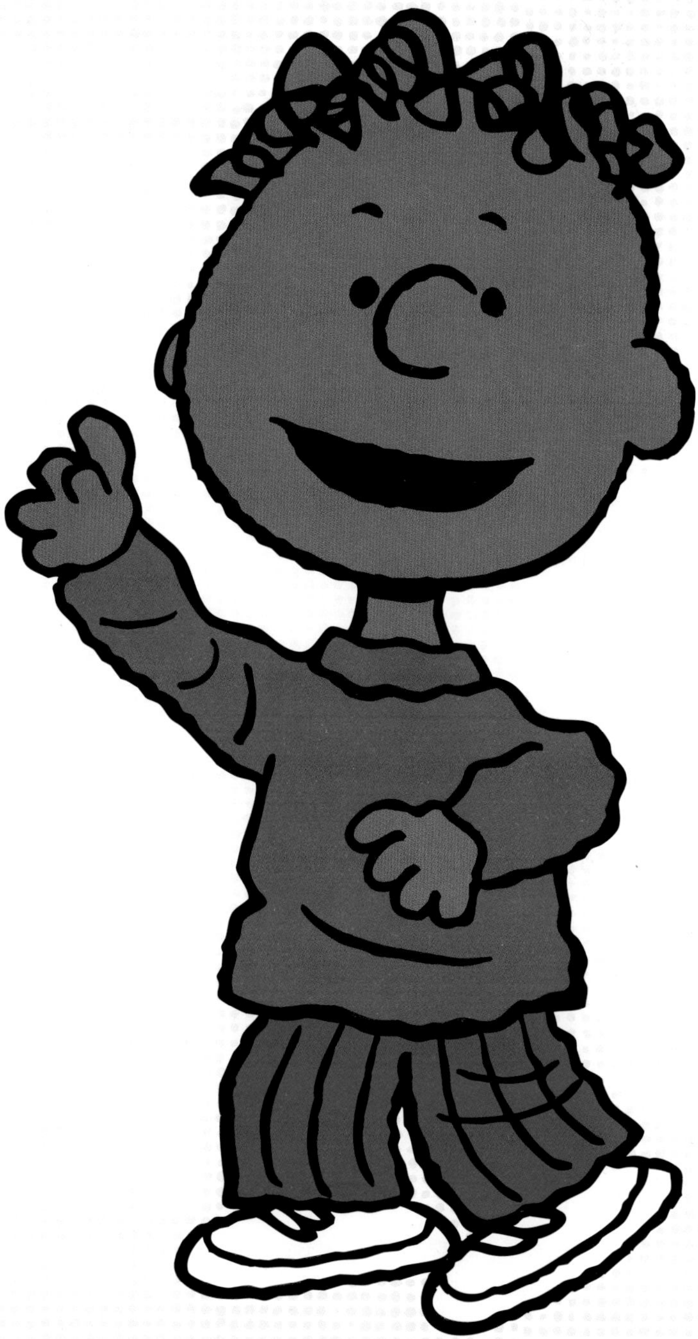

CATCHPHRASE

"My grampa says . . ."

DID YOU KNOW

• Franklin sits one seat ahead of Peppermint Patty in class.

• Franklin and Charlie Brown first met at the beach, and Franklin helped Charlie Brown fix his crooked sand castle.

LIKES AND DISLIKES
LIKES

Getting Compliments: Especially when they're sincere.

PEANUTS — I GOT SIX COMPLIMENTS TODAY... | FANTASTIC! | IT'S NOT OFTEN YOU CAN GET SIX COMPLIMENTS IN ONE DAY | TWO OF THEM WERE EVEN SINCERE!

Getting Good Grades: He worries a lot about schoolwork, but usually does well.

PEANUTS — I WORRIED ABOUT THIS TEST ALL NIGHT.. | I WORRIED AND WORRIED AND WORRIED... | SO WHAT HAPPENED? / I GOT AN "A" | I WASTED A GOOD WORRY!

Quoting His Grandfather's Words of Wisdom: He and Charlie Brown have this in common.

MY GRAMPA HAD ANOTHER BIRTHDAY YESTERDAY..

HE SAID," I HAVE TO ADMIT THAT THE YEARS HAVE BEEN GOOD TO ME"

" BUT THE MONTHS AND WEEKS HAVE BEEN A LITTLE RUDE! "

Extracurricular Activities: When the bell rings, his afternoons are booked solid!

PEANUTS
HOW ABOUT A GAME OF MARBLES AFTER SCHOOL, FRANKLIN?

I CAN'T.. I HAVE A GUITAR LESSON AT THREE-THIRTY...

RIGHT AFTER THAT I HAVE LITTLE LEAGUE, AND THEN SWIM CLUB, AND THEN DINNER AND THEN A '4-H' MEETING

I LEAD A VERY ACTIVE TUESDAY!

DISLIKES

When His Friends Act Strangely:

PEANUTS
FRANKLIN! WHERE ARE YOU GOING?

I'M GOING HOME, CHARLIE BROWN.. THIS NEIGHBORHOOD HAS ME SHOOK

I DIDN'T MIND THE GIRL IN THE BOOTH OR THE BEAGLE WITH THE GOGGLES, BUT THAT BUSINESS ABOUT THE "GREAT PUMPKIN".....NO, SIR!
BUT..

HI! DID YOU GUYS KNOW THERE ARE ONLY SIXTY MORE DAYS UNTIL BEETHOVEN'S BIRTHDAY?
OH, GOOD GRIEF!
I LIKE WOW!

Schulz Says:

"IN CONTRAST WITH THE OTHER CHARACTERS, FRANKLIN HAS THE FEWEST ANXIETIES AND OBSESSIONS."

PIGPEN

Happily traveling in his own private dust storm, Pigpen is completely comfortable in his own skin. Despite his outward appearance, he always holds his head high. Pigpen is an archaeologist in the making, and if there's a pile of dirt around, he will be in it! He appreciates the finer things in life, like soot, dust, mud, and grime. Pigpen long ago gave up worrying about such petty concerns . . . and small wonder, since he's kept cool by several layers of clay. Although the rest of the Peanuts gang sometimes questions his habits, Pigpen proceeds as if having his own private dust storm is the most natural thing in the world. His position speaks volumes for those who get picked on for their differences: If it doesn't bother him, why should it bother anybody else?

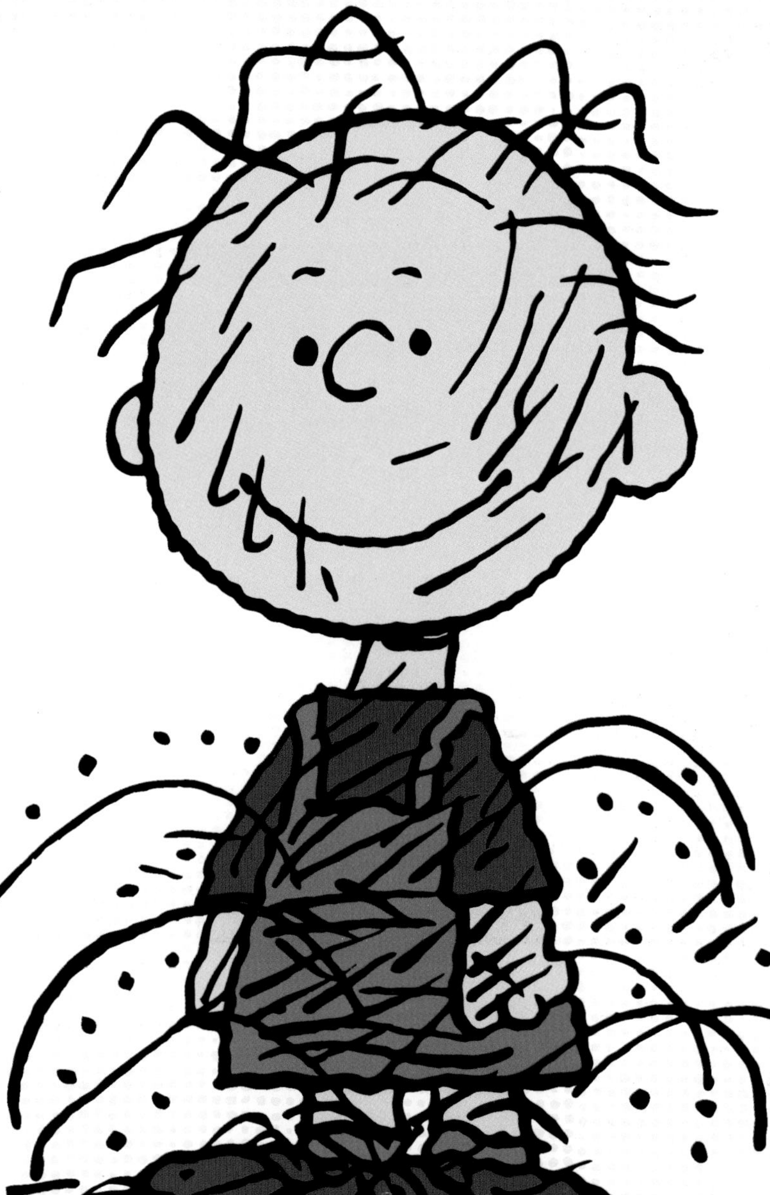

CATCHPHRASE

"I'm a dust magnet!"

Schulz Says:

"PIGPEN IS A HUMAN SOIL BANK WHO RAISES A CLOUD OF DUST ON A PERFECTLY CLEAN STREET AND PASSES OUT GUM DROPS THAT ARE INVARIABLY BLACK."

PIGPEN
THROUGH THE AGES

"I NOW HAVE TWENTY CHARACTERS, BUT THERE ARE REALLY ONLY SIX. I HAVE NOT GIVEN THE OTHERS DEPTH ENOUGH TO MAKE THEM REALLY USEFUL. PIGPEN, FOR INSTANCE. HE'S ONLY GOOD WHEN HE'S DIRTY. AND I DON'T THINK ABOUT LITTLE BOYS WHO NEED A BATH ALL THAT MUCH."

—Charles Schulz

1950s

DID YOU KNOW

• Charlie Brown is the one kid who usually accepts Pigpen for who he is, even defending his uncleanliness, and apologizing when he gives Pigpen a hard time.

• Pigpen actually took a shower in the comic strip on November 24, 1959. This is how he looks, all cleaned up:

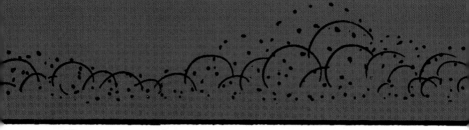

1960s   1970s   1980s   1990s

LIKES AND DISLIKES

LIKES

Giving Out Gum Drops: It's a nice gesture, but since they usually are dirty, black gum drops, his friends don't usually eat them.

Being Dirty: He sees the bright side in a having a dirty face!

Archaeology: He likes to think he's carrying the dust of civilizations around with him.

DISLIKES

Getting Clean: It has happened. It just doesn't last long.

THE LITTLE RED-HAIRED GIRL

She is the girl whose face is never seen in the comic strip . . . but who has stolen Charlie Brown's heart. He doesn't have the courage to ask her name, but he's hopelessly in love with her. She seems to know he exists but never says hello. Is she just toying with his affections? Is she cruel? We may never know. But even though Linus, Marcie, and other characters talk with her over the years, Charlie Brown has never had the courage to say hello before his nerves get the best of him and he faints, blushes, or runs away.

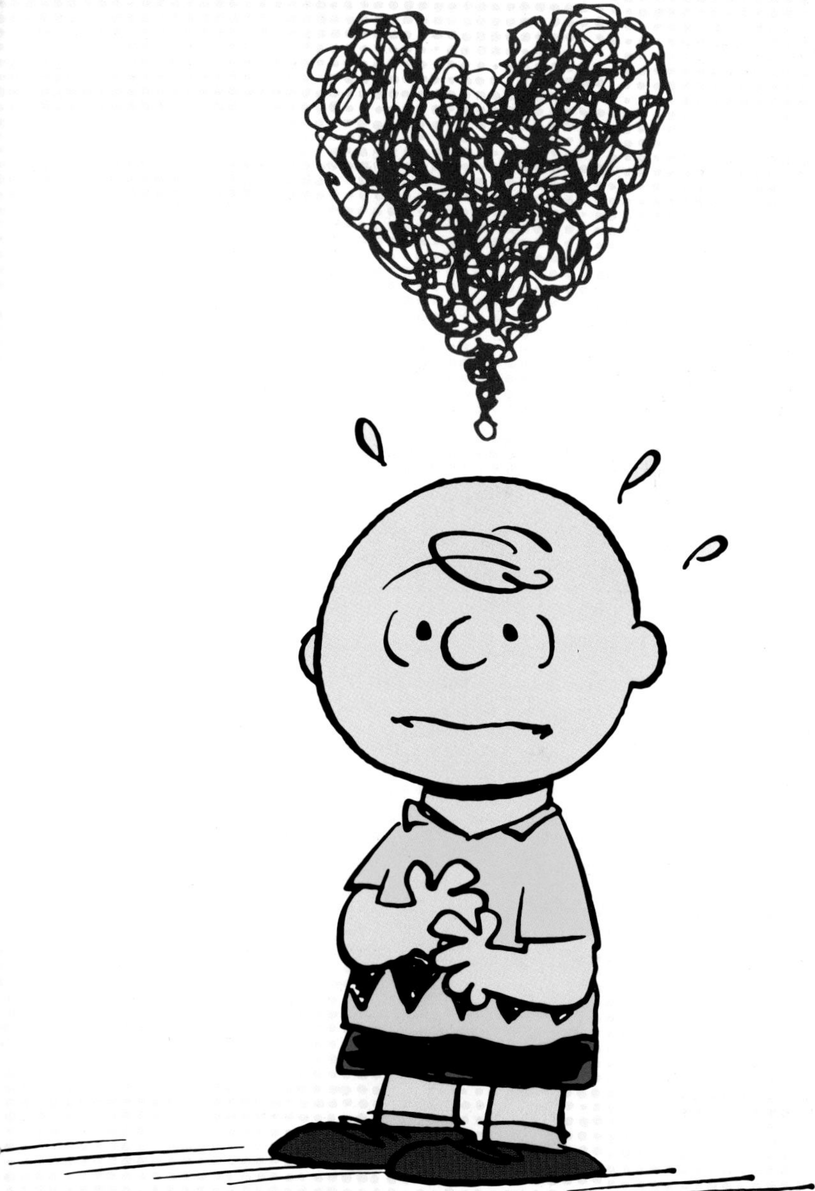

DID YOU KNOW

• Her face is never shown in the comic strip, but her silhouette was shown for the first time in the comic strip in 1999.

• She nibbles on her pencil. That's one of the few signs Charlie Brown has that she's human.

PEANUTS WHAT'S THIS? THAT LITTLE RED-HAIRED GIRL DROPPED HER PENCIL... | GEE...IT'S GOT TEETH MARKS ALL OVER IT... | SHE NIBBLES ON HER PENCIL... | SHE'S HUMAN!

• She briefly moved away from the neighborhood, causing Charlie Brown to have his life without her flash before his eyes.

PEANUTS THAT LITTLE RED-HAIRED GIRL IS GOING TO MOVE AWAY! | I'VE NEVER EVEN TALKED TO HER! I THOUGHT I HAD PLENTY OF TIME... I THOUGHT I COULD WAIT UNTIL THE SIXTH-GRADE SWIM PARTY OR THE SEVENTH-GRADE CLASS PARTY... | OR I THOUGHT I COULD ASK HER TO THE SENIOR PROM OR LOTS OF OTHER THINGS WHEN WE GOT OLDER, BUT NOW SHE'S MOVING AWAY AND IT'S TOO LATE! IT'S TOO LATE! | YOU'VE GOT TO SAY GOODBY TO HER, CHARLIE BROWN! | I'VE NEVER EVEN SAID **HELLO** TO HER!!

THE "LITTLE RED-HAIRED GIRL" EFFECT

We don't know much about the Little Red-Haired Girl, but we do know what Charlie Brown thinks about her. He can't hide it! When he sees or thinks about her . . .

He Loses His Appetite:

He Gets Nervous:

He Falls Off a Chairlift:

He Blushes:

He Strikes Out:

He Gets Very Excited . . . Only to Be Crushed Moments Later:

But not everyone feels the same way about the Little Red-Haired Girl:

Peppermint Patty sees Her as the Competition:

Lucy Feels Threatened by Her:

WOODSTOCK

Woodstock is a little yellow bird who is Snoopy's best friend, sidekick, and confidant. Whether it's as faithful mechanic to the World War I Flying Ace, loyal secretary to the Head Beagle, or root beer drinking buddy on New Year's Eve, Woodstock is never far from Snoopy's side, and they wouldn't have it any other way. In a world dominated by larger creatures—both on two legs and on four—Woodstock depends on Snoopy for protection. We never learn what species of bird Woodstock is, but he doesn't behave like a regular bird. With Snoopy's help, he doesn't have to fly south for the winter or do what other birds do. The closest he gets to flying south is diving into Snoopy's water bowl. He's a special little bird!

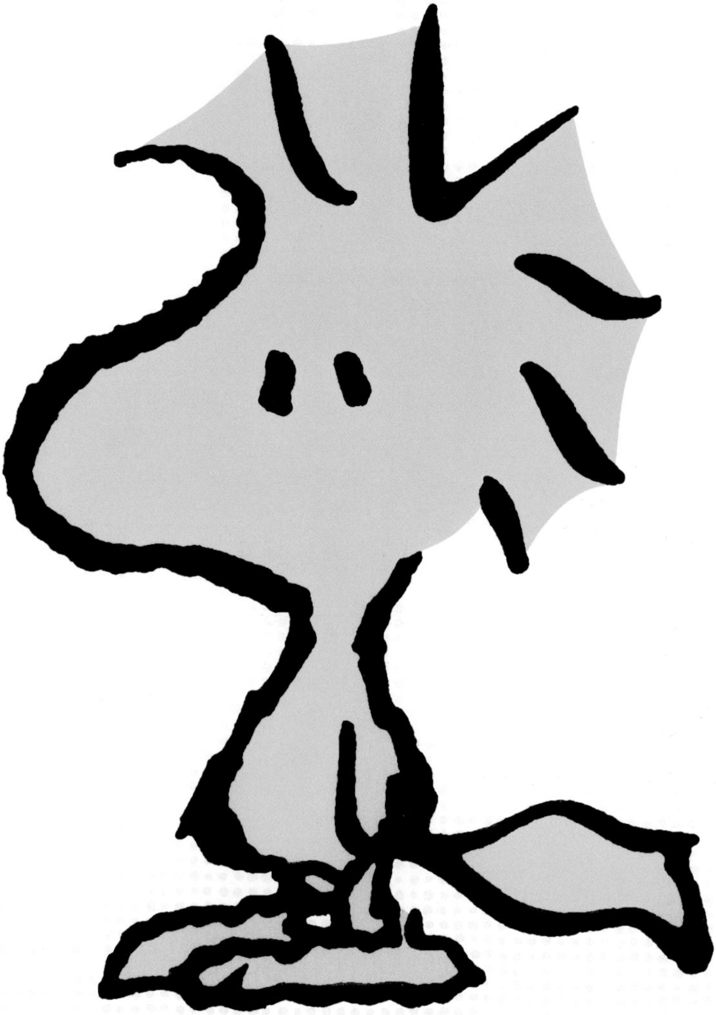

DID YOU KNOW

- Woodstock was first seen in the strip in 1967, as an unnamed bird who often flew upside down. He didn't get named until 1970, after the Woodstock music festival.

- He speaks in a language only Snoopy understands.

- Woodstock can often be seen sleeping on Snoopy's belly.

LIKES AND DISLIKES
LIKES

His Nest: There's no place like home!

His Friend Snoopy: Snoopy protects Woodstock in every way he can.

Worms: Unlike other birds, Woodstock has crushes on worms instead of eating them.

DISLIKES

Snoopy, When He Teases Him: Do not try this at home!

Having to Be Careful Because He's Small:

Schulz Says:

"WOODSTOCK KNOWS THAT HE IS VERY SMALL AND INCONSEQUENTIAL INDEED. IT'S A PROBLEM WE ALL HAVE. THE UNIVERSE BOGGLES US. IN THE LARGER SCHEME, WE SUDDENLY REALIZE, WE AMOUNT TO VERY LITTLE. . . . WOODSTOCK IS A LIGHTHEARTED EXPRESSION OF THAT IDEA."

THE BEAGLE SCOUTS

For the first few years of the comic strip, Woodstock was the only yellow bird in the Peanuts universe. This changed when Snoopy became a Beagle Scout Master, leading a flock of Woodstock's little buddies. The Beagle Scouts are named Bill, Olivier, Harriet, Raymond (the purple one), Conrad, Fred, and Roy. They joined Snoopy on his outdoor adventures, served as ground crew for the Flying Ace's plane (Snoopy's doghouse, that is), and were members of Snoopy's pirate crew!

DID YOU KNOW

- Bill and Harriet got married.
- Harriet is famous for her angel food cake with seven-minute frosting.

LIKES AND DISLIKES

LIKES

Their Leader, Snoopy: They want to be just like him.

Hiking: That's what being a scout is all about.

DISLIKES

Snakes: Sometimes the Beagle Scouts have trouble with proper scout behavior, like when there is a snake nearby.

SNOOPY'S SIBLINGS

Snoopy has one sister, Belle, and four brothers, all born at the Daisy Hill Puppy Farm. They were separated for a long time after they left the farm. Then Charlie Brown helped Snoopy by writing a letter to the owners, asking them to track down Snoopy's siblings. Soon Snoopy reunited with them. Snoopy sees Spike pretty often, even though he lives far away in the desert, but Snoopy doesn't see his sister and other brothers as much. When they do visit Snoopy, you can easily tell them apart by their appearance: Spike has whiskers and a wide-brimmed hat, Olaf is a bit chubby, Marbles has spots, Andy has shaggy fur, and Belle has eyelashes.

PEANUTS

DAISY HILL PUPPY FARM
DEAR SIR,
I AM WRITING IN BEHALF
OF MY DOG SNOOPY.

HE WOULD LIKE TO GET IN TOUCH WITH SOME OF HIS BROTHERS AND SISTERS WHOM HE HASN'T SEEN SINCE LEAVING YOUR PLACE.

I AM ENCLOSING HIS PAPERS SO YOU WILL KNOW WHAT LITTER HE WAS FROM.
SINCERELY,
CHARLIE BROWN

I CAN HARDLY WAIT... WE'LL HAVE AN OLD-FASHIONED LITTER REUNION!

SPIKE

Spike has lived alone in the desert for so long that he holds conversations with tumbleweeds and cactus plants. (Fortunately, they don't talk back to him.) Snoopy's quite fond of Spike and more than once has tried to find him a home in the neighborhood, but Spike's really too much of a solitary soul to enjoy being around too many people.

Schulz Says:

"SPIKE, SNOOPY'S BROTHER, IS A BEAUTIFUL EXAMPLE OF IMAGES EVOKED BY A LOCATION: WE KNOW HE LIVES WITH THE COYOTES OUTSIDE NEEDLES, AND THAT'S ABOUT ALL WE KNOW. THERE IS ABOUT HIM, WITH HIS THIN, FAINTLY EXOTIC MUSTACHE AND SOULFUL EYES, AN AIR OF MYSTERY THAT IS TOTALLY FOREIGN TO WHAT SNOOPY IS. OUR IMAGINATION TAKES OVER."

ANDY

Andy is another of Snoopy's brothers and refers to himself as a simple farm dog. Known for his shaggy appearance, Andy is never far from Olaf's side, and the two enjoy traveling together.

MARBLES

Marbles is another of Snoopy's brothers and is known for being "the smart one in the family." Marbles is an observer who dabbles in the occasional research project. He's easily identified by his spots.

BELLE

Snoopy's only sister, Belle, lives in Kansas City. She is not quite as eccentric as her brothers, though she has been known to play a Red Cross Nurse when Snoopy imagines being the Flying Ace.

OLAF

Snoopy's chubby brother, Olaf, was once entered into an "ugly dog contest" and won. Olaf is beautiful on the inside, though, and rushed to Snoopy's bedside when Snoopy was sick with pneumonia.

SHERMY

One of the original four characters in the comic strip along with Patty, Charlie Brown, and Snoopy, Shermy is one of Charlie Brown's earliest friends. Shermy is easygoing and dependable. He always gets the best toys at Christmas too.

PATTY

Another one of the original four characters in the comic strip, Patty is best friends with Violet. The two of them can often be found playing together (which sometimes means tormenting Charlie Brown).

VIOLET

Violet was the second girl to be introduced into Peanuts. She is best friends with Patty. Violet likes to make mud pies and sell them to her best customer, PigPen.

FRIEDA

Known for her "naturally curly hair" and her cat, Faron, Frieda plays outfield on Charlie Brown's baseball team, though she would much rather plant flowers on his pitcher's mound or get Snoopy to chase rabbits like a real dog.

EUDORA

Eudora is Sally's best friend, and the pair make quite a team at summer camp. Like Sally, Eudora has a unique outlook on the world and sometimes competes for Linus's affection (or maybe she just wants his blanket).

PEGGY JEAN

Peggy Jean met Charlie Brown at summer camp (she calls him "Brownie Charles"), and the two became pen pals. Innocent and endearing, Peggy Jean is one of the few people who likes Charlie Brown just the way he is.

OTHER FRIENDS IN THE NEIGHBORHOOD

These other characters make occasional appearances in the Peanuts world:

5 and his twin sisters **3** and **4** were bizarrely named after their zip code. 5 can sometimes be seen on the ball field with Charlie Brown, and 3 and 4 are best known for their dancing in the animated special *A Charlie Brown Christmas*.

Faron is Frieda's limp-boned cat who doesn't do much of anything but hang in her arms.

Austin, Ruby, Leland, and **Milo** are part of a Little League team called the Goose Eggs, who Charlie Brown once managed.

Crybaby Boobie is a terror on the tennis court, not because of her skills but because of her incessant whining.

Bad Call Benny is Crybaby's tennis partner—while she whines, he insults his opponents and makes one bad call after another.

Molley Volley is the loudmouthed tennis partner Snoopy gets saddled with.

Joe Richkid is a stuck-up golfer who goes head-to-head in a tournament with Peppermint Patty, Marcie, and the Masked Marvel (Snoopy).

José Peterson is the best slugger on Peppermint Patty's baseball team.

Clara, Shirley, and **Sophie** are an inseparable trio of girls who met at Camp Kamp. Their counselor was Peppermint Patty.

Emily met Charlie Brown at a ballroom dance class. She once asked him to the Sweetheart Ball!

Cormac wants to grow up to be a ladies' man and practices his smooth moves on Sally, who is completely uninterested.

Thibault is a short and grouchy player on Peppermint Patty's baseball team.

Tapioca Pudding is a girl whose father wants to license her likeness onto anything and everything!

Harold Angel is a classmate of Sally's and another one of her many admirers.

Loretta is a Girl Scout who Snoopy met on one of his long Beagle Scout hikes.

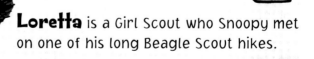

Lydia is a girl who Linus has a crush on, and Lydia thinks he is much too old for her.

Roy is a schoolmate of Peppermint Patty and a pal of Charlie Brown, who he met at summer camp.

Poochie knows Snoopy from his days on the Daisy Hill Puppy Farm. She was the first to play fetch with him.

Naomi nursed a sick Spike back to health at her mother's vet clinic.

Maynard was once Peppermint Patty's tutor.

Royanne is the granddaughter of Roy Hobbs and a pitcher on an opposing team, and she develops a crush on Charlie Brown.

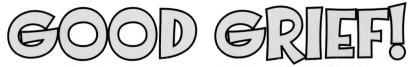

GOOD GRIEF!

Did you know there were so many Peanuts characters? As Charlie Brown likes to say, "Good grief!"

Now that you've met most of the Peanuts gang, maybe it's time for you to add *yourself* to the picture. Have you ever thought about what you would look like as a Peanuts character? Take out a piece of paper, and get drawing!

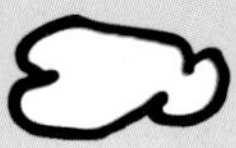

CONTENTS

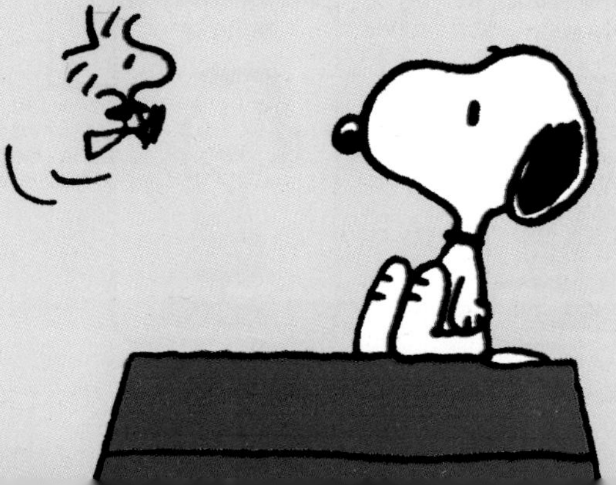

PEANUTS FAMILY TREE

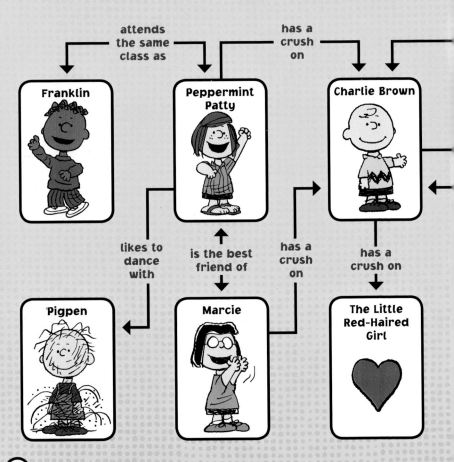

attends the same class as

has a crush on

Franklin

Peppermint Patty

Charlie Brown

likes to dance with

is the best friend of

has a crush on

has a crush on

Pigpen

Marcie

The Little Red-Haired Girl